P9-DFF-690

I Love You, Little One

NANCY TAFURI

Scholastic Press • *New York*

Haverstraw King's Daughters
Public Library
10 W. Ramapo Road
Garnerville, NY 10923

Copyright © 1998 by Nancy Tafuri

All rights reserved. Published by Scholastic Press,

a division of Scholastic Inc. SCHOLASTIC PRESS and colophon are trademarks of Scholastic Inc.

For information regarding permissions, write to Scholastic Inc.,

Attention: Permissions Department, 555 Broadway, New York, New York 10012.

LIBRARY OF CONGRESS CATALOGING-IN-PUBLICATION DATA

Tafuri, Nancy.   I love you, little one / Nancy Tafuri.   p. cm.

Summary: Mama animals tell their little ones all the ways they are loved, forever and always.

ISBN 0-590-92159-2   [1. Animals — Infancy — Fiction. 2. Mother and child — Fiction.]

I. Title   PZ7.T117Iaan 1997   [E] — dc20 96-30791   CIP   AC

Book design by David Saylor

The artwork was created with watercolor inks and colored pencils.

The text is set in 22-point Iowan Bold Italic.

10   9   8   7   02   03

FIRST EDITION, MARCH 1998

Printed in Mexico   49

For Cristina, my little one,
and for Lauren Thompson and Owen,
her little one

Deep in the woods
by the sandy riverbank,
a little deer asks,
"Do you love me, Mama?"

And Mama Deer says,
"Yes, little one,
I love you as the river loves you,
full and singing before you,
giving you cool water to drink.
I love you as the river loves you,
forever and ever and always."

Deep in the woods
by the mossy pond edge,
a little duck asks,
"Do you love me, Mama?"

And Mama Duck says,
"Yes, little one,
I love you as the pond loves you,
wide and calm beneath you,
giving you food and places to swim.
I love you as the pond loves you,
forever and ever and always."

Deep in the woods
in a dirt-dug burrow,
a little rabbit asks,
"Do you love me, Mama?"

And Mama Rabbit says,
"Yes, little one,
I love you as the earth loves you,
cozy and snug around you,
giving you a warm place to sleep.
I love you as the earth loves you,
forever and ever and always."

Haverstraw King's Daughters
Public Library

Deep in the woods
in a grassy meadow,
a little mouse asks,
"Do you love me, Mama?"

And Mama Mouse says,
"Yes, little one,
I love you as the wild rye loves you,
gently swaying above you,
giving you food and cover from harm.
I love you as the wild rye loves you,
forever and ever and always."

Deep in the woods
in a dark mountain cave,
a little bear asks,
"Do you love me, Mama?"

And Mama Bear says,
"Yes, little one,
   I love you as the mountain loves you,
   sturdy and safe around you,
   giving you shelter from snow and rain.
   I love you as the mountain loves you,
   forever and ever and always."

Deep in the woods
in an oak tree hollow,
a little owl asks,
"Do you love me, Mama?"

And Mama Owl says,
"Yes, little one,
I love you as the oak tree loves you,
tall and strong beside you,
giving you the world to see all around.
I love you as the oak tree loves you,
forever and ever and always."

Deep in the woods
in a log-built house,
a little child asks,
"Do you love me, Mama?"

And Mama says,
"Yes, little one,
I love you as the stars love you,
constant and bright above you,
giving you joy and peace and wonder.
I love you as the stars love you,
                    forever,
                            and ever,
                                    and always."